THE POWER OF JUDGE NAUGHT

Diane M Scabilloni

Illustrated by:
Michele Katz

Edited by:
Laura Hill

First Edition

The Power of Judge Naught

Diane M Scabilloni

ISBN: 9798519721561
Self Published
Bethel Park, PA

ON MY HEART....

I am grateful for:

The pings
The spiritual images
The promptings
The signs that I am on the right track
The synchronicities
The knowings
Imagination
An open heart
Creativity
Being a vessel of His special message
Collaboration
Blessings Beyond Measure
God's enduring Love

Thank you to my family of "Inspirers" and "Encouragers". You know who you are and you are deeply loved. Your support and love keep me moving forward with God's will in my life.

Inspirational Scriptures:

Trust in the Lord with all your heart
and lean not on your own understanding;
in all your ways submit to him,
and he will make your paths straight.
Proverbs 3:5-6

Fill your thoughts with heavenly realities, and not with the distractions of the natural realm.
Colossians 3:2

Don't be pulled into different directions or worried about a thing.
Tell him every detail of your life,
then God's wonderful peace that transcends human understanding,
will guard your heart and mind through Jesus Christ.
Philippians 4:6-8

And I will ask the Father, and he will give you another advocate to help you and be with you forever—the Spirit of Truth. The world cannot accept him, because it neither sees him or knows him. But you know him, for he lives with you and will be in you.
John 14: 16-17

When God created my spirit,
we had a magical conversation
about who I was to become.

He was preparing me for my
journey to earth.

God looked into my eyes with love and said, "I have special promises I want you to remember while on your journey. Allow the beauty of my words to sink into your heart and keep them there forever. Always remember:

"You are powerfully loved.

You have special gifts to share with the world.

I am always with you to guide and protect you."

God shared, "On your journey, you will have experiences that will challenge you to forget these promises. I encourage you to persist in *knowing* the promises are *for you.* No matter what happens, the promises will *remain with you.*"

Knowing my journey would have challenges, God wanted me to have a constant reminder of my special promises. So He introduced me to Judge Naught. As soon as I met Judge Naught I knew he had a kind and loving heart. I could tell he had much wisdom to share.

God revealed how Judge Naught would have a special assignment in my life. God lovingly explained to me:

"Judge Naught will help you focus your thoughts on your beautiful God given promises.

Judge Naught will be your defender.

Judge Naught will empower and comfort you on your journey."

Now, I want to share some of my Judge Naught stories with you. He makes such an impact on the flow and beauty of my life.

One day, I was next door playing at my best friend's house. We had an argument. She yelled at me and said, "I do not like you. And as a matter of fact, no one else likes you either."

"What a terrible day!" I mumbled to myself as I walked home. All afternoon, I kept thinking of my friend's words and it made me feel sad and hurt.

As I sat in my bedroom feeling lonely, I noticed a tapping in my heart, "BAM, BAM, BAM!" It was Judge Naught. He was in the chambers at his judge's desk. He grabbed his gavel and with a big swing "BAM BAM BAM!" He said, "Judge Not! The Promise is, you are powerfully loved by the CREATOR OF THE UNIVERSE!" I let that promise sink in my heart. I knew it was true. I felt a calm come over me. I felt loved and accepted by God.

Another time, I was talking with a friend. He was telling me about a problem he was having with his parents. I listened to him, asked questions, and shared my thoughts. I encouraged him to know that it would all work out. With a big smile, my friend said, "You are so good at listening and helping people feel better. What a special gift you have!" I knew I was enjoying my time with him but I did not think I was using a special gift.

Suddenly, I felt a tapping in my heart, "BAM, BAM, BAM!" It was Judge Naught. He was in the chambers at his judge's desk. He grabbed his gavel and with a big swing "BAM BAM BAM!" He said, "Judge Not! The Promise is, you have unique gifts and talents to share with the world. You were created with a purpose." I let that promise sink in my heart. I knew it was true. He whispered, "What comes easily with peace and joy are gifts from God!"

Another time, I had to write a speech for school. Part of the assignment was to present it to the class. I spent a lot of time on the project. I did a lot of research on my topic and was well prepared.

While standing in front of the classroom to present my speech, and knowing the teacher would be grading me, I started to worry that no one would like my work. Then I thought, "What if I mess up?"

I got super nervous. I felt my face get red and the palms of my hands started to sweat.

Before I knew it, I felt a tapping in my heart, "BAM, BAM, BAM!" It was Judge Naught. He was in the chambers at his judge's desk. He grabbed his gavel and with a big swing "BAM BAM BAM!" He said, "Judge Not! The Promise is, you are always guided and protected by God." I took a deep breath and released a long sigh. I let that promise sink in my heart. I knew it was true. I felt a sense of peace and excitement come over me. I presented my speech with confidence and joy!

So, these are just a few of my Judge Naught stories. In my imagination, I often give Judge Naught a high five for the wisdom he shares and the peace and joy he brings to my life. He helps me to see the world the way God sees it. I now know that is the best way.

Because of Judge Naught's guidance, I have learned that while things will happen that I do not like, no matter what, I will hold onto these Promises:

I am powerfully loved.

I have special gifts to share with the world.

God is always with me to guide and protect me.

I am so grateful to have Judge Naught as my protector and friend to "BAM BAM BAM!" my heart with God's special promises and fasten them there for safekeeping.

THANK YOU JUDGE NAUGHT!

If you loved this book,
You will also love:

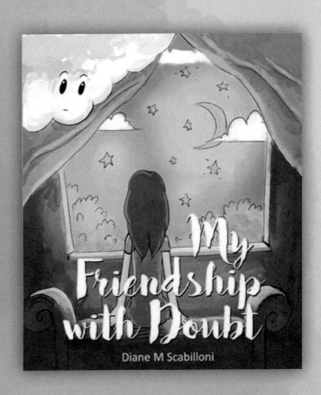

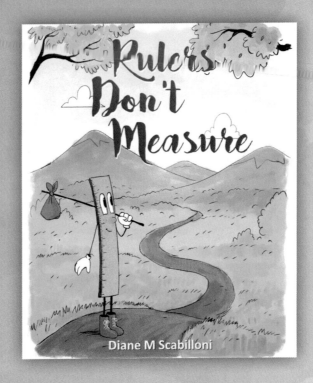

Available for purchase at:

www.amazon.com

Or visit

🌐 www.dianescabilloni.com

f @dianescabilloniauthor

📷 @dianescabilloniauthor

▶ Diane Scabilloni

Made in the USA
Middletown, DE
16 October 2023